MCDOOGLE'S MONSTER FARM

The Day the Gogglynipper Escaped

Written by James McKnight
Illustrated by Mark Chambers

Licensed exclusively to Top That Publishing Ltd
Tide Mill Way, Woodbridge, Suffolk, IP12 1AP, UK
www.topthatpublishing.com
Concept & text copyright © 2012 James McKnight
Illustrations copyright © 2012 Mark Chambers
All rights reserved
2 4 6 8 9 7 5 3 1
Manufactured in China

Written by James McKnight
Illustrated by Mark Chambers

ISBN 978-1-78244-014-7

A catalogue record for this book is available from the British Library

One day, Diggle was out on the hillside blowing his special whistle, rounding up the Gogglynippers.

His trusty dog Noober helped him bring in all the Gogglynippers, rounding them up one by one, and herding them into their enclosure.

Diggle counted the Gogglynippers, 'One, two, three, four, five, six, seven, eight, nine ...
Only nine Gogglynippers! Oh no!' said Diggle.
'We're missing a Gogglynipper!'

How was Diggle going to tell Farmer McDoogle that he had lost a Gogglynipper, the biggest, scariest monster on the farm?

Diggle decided that he had to find the missing Gogglynipper before it got dark. He headed up into the hills with his trusty dog, Noober.

Diggle searched up and down the hills, blowing on his special whistle as hard as he could. As it got darker, Noober began to get scared, and howled along with Diggle's whistle.

Suddenly, Diggle slipped on a big pile of mud and fell onto his bottom with a squelch. 'Hang on a minute,' thought Diggle, 'this pile of mud smells very bad.' Diggle knew of only one thing that could smell that bad …

Yuck

... Gogglynipper poo! A big, steaming pile of Gogglynipper poo! A clue!

Then, Diggle spotted some enormous footprints, made by an enormous foot with three enormous toes.

Diggle followed the footprints into a big cave. He edged slowly and carefully into the cave as he knew that Gogglynippers are not only the biggest monsters, they are also the most dramatic.

Suddenly, there was a big, loud roar and the Gogglynipper came running out of the cave.

He ran right up to Diggle, opened his mouth wide and licked him from top to bottom! (What Diggle didn't know is that even the biggest monsters can be scared of the dark, so the Gogglynipper was very happy to see him.)

Diggle attached a lead
to the Gogglynipper
and began the journey
back to the farm to
put the monster to bed.

Diggle could hear all of the other monsters snoring very loudly, even though he was very far away over the hills. (Monsters snore very loudly.)

When they were halfway home, the Gogglynipper started to act strangely. He sniffed the air and got very excited. Then he started jumping up and down, and began to pull on his lead. Diggle suddenly noticed a smell in the air. It was the smell of very smelly old socks. (Gogglynippers love eating very smelly old socks!)

Yum!

Yum!

Woof! Woof!

The Gogglynipper sped off in the direction that the smell was coming from. 'Nooooooooo!' screamed Diggle, as he was pulled along, hanging onto the end of the lead. Noober chased after them barking!

The Gogglynipper did not slow down for a second. He dragged Diggle up and down one hill and then up and down another.

Help!

They raced faster and faster!
Diggle couldn't even see what
direction they were going.

Soon they arrived back
at the farm. The Gogglynipper
raced straight past the monster enclosure,
round the corner to the farmhouse, and
straight up to the farmhouse window.

Hanging out of the window were two very large, very smelly old socks!

Just as the Gogglynipper was about to bite the two very large feet, they disappeared and Farmer McDoogle stuck his head out of the window! 'What do you think you're doing with that Gogglynipper?' he said.

Once Diggle explained what had happened, Farmer McDoogle laughed and said, 'It's a good job I only wash my socks once a week!'

Pongy Socks

Farmer McDoogle helped Diggle put the Gogglynipper into the enclosure with the other monsters, and they all went to bed. After washing their socks, of course.